The Magic of an IDEA

By Raul Barios

When you the reader-read this story, I want to let you know this story comes from a vision.

This vision (A woman).

Gave me a pretty good idea for the next book.

For those out there in the real world, sadly my approach was the opposite of the reaction I got from her, and we never got to meet?

But the silver lining to this story?

I thank you for the inspiration for another great book in my collections of books!

Hope you the reader-get to enjoy this story as much as I got to enjoy writing it.

Now, cue the story, enjoy the show reader!

Retail Can Be Fun

Working the self-checkout today, I always was amazed at how people were such in a hurry to scan their-crap through.

And then when the next person rolls in behind them, I have too-stop-the next person coming into the station; that person trying to scan and nothing was scanning and I have too-tell the customer; "Sir or Mam, you have to wait until the station resets!"

And they stare you at you like you
are crazy, because you just ruined
there moment, as they look at you,
crazy at the fact that-they were in a
hurry!

Having to do this a lot, I realized
people were in a hurry all the dam
time!

But I liked working self-checkout.

My brother Tony would come in
my lines when I was working them-
before getting off work.

He would make a scene in front of
other people and ask me these
stupid questions like; "What's the
price check?"

Or say; "Where did these eggs
come from?"
Or say; "Why does this machine not
accept the card?"

He was doing this on purpose!

I loved my brother Tony.

He was always funny like that.

I been working here at Mr. Pete's
Groceries for almost six years!

I started working as a cashier, bored
one day, I asked my cashier
manager in charge, Samantha.

How about teaching me how to do
self-checkout or learn the customer
service side of things, I ask her.

She says okay and just like that-I
learned the three jobs!

Tonight, my brother stops in my
self-checkout line, messing with me
of course, before letting anyone
know around us-he was my brother.

Then he stops to talk to me; telling
me about his security job and
telling me about how another idiot-
tried to storm in the government
building he worked at in Seattle.

"We had to take the sucker down!"
Explaining the details to me.

So, what was the ending result of
the situation?

"We had to tackle him down and
hold him in a chair until Seattle PD
was able to take him in for
unauthorized entry into the
building."

What brings you here tonight
brother?

"I am here tonight because I needed
some more whip cream," Looking
at his bag, trying to not think what
he was planning to use that whip
cream for?

"I know what you are thinking brother," Tony seeing right through me.

"I am using this for the short cake I bought, so I could share it with my dog, brother."

Laughing at this because my mind was going in other directions.

Sorry for thinking weird brother, I apologize.

"You should start dating again!" Saying this bluntly to me.

I do not want to date right now.

"Why not?"

"When was your last date, do you even remember that?"

I do remember the last date I had.

"When was it?"

It was two months ago!

"Do you remember her name?"

Yes, I do!

Cindy Sherill.

"The crazy fantasy girl!" Tony says
laughing.

She was not crazy!

She was just weird about stuff, and
I did not want to go-out with her
anymore.

"But you were having sex with her!"

"Was she weird in bed or something?"

Nothing like that brother.

Cindy, Cindy, Cindy, I tell my thoughts.

Our first date, which all first dates to me were called the interview process, because to me, the first date, you are meeting each other, and to me, it was like being on a job interview.

Cindy, I had met online.

I remember the date well-February 16th.

The only reason I remember the date well- because it was a few days after Valentine's Day- and I had nobody this year or the last year.

This was only the reason of remembering the date so well.

Online, she had this picture of her eyes-just staring at the photo, as if she was looking into your soul, it seemed like to me.

She had this paw print on top of her chest and that filled out her picture for the profile.

I said hello, and she responded within an hour with a hello back.

Talking to her about nothing, just talking about what do you do and what do you like; the ice breaker conversations, where they were short and sweet because come on guys!

You are not the only one talking to
this girl!

Every guy wishing for a message
from a female, might be lucky and
get 1 message, where a woman can
get about 50 to 100 a day.

The numbers were never in it-for
the guy's favor!

I considered myself lucky, lucky
she was easy to chat with.

It took two days of chatting back
and forth, the day of the date, she
gave me her number and we texted.

On the drive to our date in Seattle; I
was taking her to this sushi
restaurant I heard about online
when I searched online for a nice
sushi place in Seattle.

Before going on our date-she told
me how she liked serial killers and
how she liked horror movies!

In my head I was like; oh, oh-okay?

On the drive there I took a detour
and showed her a couple places
where some serial killers in our
state-did their prowling's in.

I am not going to tell you, the
reader here, on who they were?

When inside the sushi place, it was
dim-lighted, very colorful, etc.

We chatted on and on about
anything.

She had just moved here four
months prior, leaving the state of
Oregon.

She moved in with her brother and
his wife and there two kids and
their three dogs.

The funny part about this interview
/ date, she leans into me from her
side of the table asking me next;
"What is your fantasy?"

Myself, never asked this question, I
said without thinking; "I would like
to see what a second date looked
like?" Smiling to myself.

She looked at me, laughing a little
to herself, realizing I was being
funny.

"Do you want to know what my
fantasy is?" She says-wondering
my thoughts?

Sure, I tell her.

"My fantasy is to run half-naked through a forest and I want Freddie, Michael, and Jason, to hack me to death!"

SHE WAS SERIOUS WHEN SAYING THIS BY THE WAY.

I looked at her surprised and I whispered to her, leaning in a little to her face; Do not ever tell anyone this!

On the drive back, she held my hand and asked if she could sleep over and I told her; I do not have bunk beds, making a joke about her comment.

We did have sex that first night of meeting.

I hate the term one night stand, because if two people meet on the first night and everything works out great!

Then what is wrong with two
people having sex the first night?

What I remember though, I
remember her riding me like she
was on a horse!

It was funny to me.

It just was!

We met six more times and it was a
great relationship, until the drugs
started.

I did not know, but before she came
here, she was really into cocaine.

I had never tried drugs in my life.

Cindy tried a lot of them!

The few times we met, she would
be twitchy, or she would be
sweating so much for no reason.

The last time I saw her, two-months
ago.

She called me out of the blue,
asking if I could pick her up
because she was at her cousins and
she was not wanting to go to her
brothers, and I think it was because
she was doing some heavy stuff that
night.
Picking her up, holding her hand
for no reason, I could feel she could
not stop shaking!

I did not say nothing, I quietly
walked her in the house, Tony was
asleep already, so he did not hear
us, when walking in.

I had my own shower in my room.

When Tony and me-bought this
house four years ago, we found a
perfect home in our city of Kent,
Washington.

The house was a three bedroom, but
within the first year of living here,

we both agreed that we should build
a bathroom in each room, for
privacy reasons and just because we
were bachelors in our late 20's.

Tony and me-have a great
relationship as brothers.

We never fight, we never argue.

The reason we bought the house
was because we wanted to make
sure we had a roof over our head
and we could save for another
house, for if we both meet our
future wives, later in life.

Cindy asked if she could take a
shower and I told her sure, giving
her a towel.

She came out after her shower, but
she was still sweating, and she was
naked in front of me; I walk her to
the side of the bed and ask her if
she was okay.

We had not seen each other for a
while now and that was because she
found someone else-she was dating,
and I did not fight for her love or
anything.

I just let her be and enjoyed the
time with her.

I got in the shower with her this
time.

I ran the cold water on both of us,
she still shaking a little.

Giving her a towel, drying her off.

Both of us naked in my bed, I hold
her, she falls asleep, not saying
anything else.

I wake up around 5am or so, she
hugs me goodbye, and I remember
her breast between her sweater she
had on, pressing against my face,
she says her cousin is outside to
pick her up.

I never saw her again!

"What are you thinking about
brother?" Tony awakening me from
my dream.

I was just thinking about Cindy,
that's all, I tell him.

I then remind him of how annoying
it was, cleaning out our jacuzzi,
when he had his friend over a few
nights ago.

"You should have seen this girl,
brother," Tony saying.
"As soon as we got in it, she took
off her clothes and we were naked,
making out in the hot tub!"

You know you-made a puddle
leading into the guest bathroom.

"I am sorry brother, but the rule is,
after you get in a jacuzzi, you have

to take a shower, and that is what
we did!"

Is that what the owner's manual
say's about the jacuzzi rules, I ask
being a smart ass.

"What ever brother," Tony starting
to walk out to the exit door.

Melissa, one of my managers, she
walks over to me saying it was time
for my ten-minute break.

I say okay, walking towards the exit
to talk to my brother once more
before he leaves.

He looks at Melissa, looking back
at me.

"Why did you not ever hit that!"
Mad at me for not making a move
on Melissa.

Because she is one of my managers
and I do not want to mix work with
pleasure.

"Does she have a boyfriend yet?"

No, she does not, I say.

"Don't you like text her every night
or so?"

We text, but we are friends and
nothing more.

My brother staring at her ass, I
could tell this and I ask him to
politely look up and not look down.

"She has a cute figure for being
short, not fat, and looking like she
can wear anything she wants, you
know?"

What you do not know brother is
that Melissa gets hit on way too
much with the weirdos here and I
am sure she is tired of being asked
for her number or being asked if

she could be some guy's sugar
baby!

"Yeah, that would suck brother,"
Tony agreeing with me.

"Oh," My brother saying, before
unlocking his door.

"We are going to a Renaissance
Fair tomorrow, out in Federal way,
by the fair grounds."

Why?
I ask wondering.

"You know how I sign up for those
big brother programs at the family
building," My brother referring to
that office where a few years ago,
he became a big brother, and he
would take young local boys out
every Saturday.

My brother loved kids, but he never
could find a woman he loved to
have kids with.

He had three long time girlfriends,
amounting to about 16yrs.

Tony is younger than me.

I am 29, Tony is 27.

I think at 25, he gave up on true
love when his last girlfriend;
Jennifer, had gotten married, two
years after they broke up.

She had invited him to the wedding,
and I advised him not to go to it,
but he did anyways!

A few months when she had moved
on, he was drunk, walking into my
bedroom-telling me how her new
boyfriend was not as good looking
as him, and I laughed, because
every guy says this, so they do not
feel as if they were dumped, I
guess.

I showed the picture of my brother
and her new man to friends, and
everyone agreed the opposite.

They were agreeing with what my
brother said and even I agreed to it,
but in the end, she is now married
to this guy, and you have to-let her
go.

He did eventually, but then he got
lost into the world of online dating
and he loved to swipe right!

I think to him-dating and not ever
being in love again, helps him cope
with his loss.

I once went inside his room a few
months ago- because he had left our
vacuum in there without putting it
back in the main hallway closet.

I noticed he still had a picture in a
frame with the two of them, when
they went rock climbing at that
place at the mall in south hill.

I think he looks at that picture and it
reminds him of what love was
really like for him, once upon a
time ago.

So, his dates he goes on with now a
days-is like the drug that fuels him
for the lust, but when he gets home,
he looks at the picture to remind
him of how once upon a time ago,
he had a love once.

Seeing couples around us, it never
gets to me much.

I see so many of them because I
work in a grocery store.

You see that one thing that nobody
really sees and that is that love
circle that people are in.

When you are not in love, you
could see the circle underneath the

couple's feet and for me, I cheer for
them all.

I think love is the greatest power
that can only be, when two people
love each other.

"Brother, are you daydreaming
right now again?"
Tony staring at me.

Sorry, I tell him.

I was just thinking about
something.

"Well, when you get off of work,
get some good sleep and we leave
at 8am sharp, for this Renaissance
Fair!" Saying, before driving away.

Romeo art Thou Romeo

"I have a funny question to ask you brother?"

Shoot, Saying without question to me.

"How many virgins do you think are here with us at this fair and how many women to men ratio, you think is here; saying the joke, just

wondering what my brother would
think?"

Oh, that is easy brother, Saying
back.

There, has to be at least one woman
per twenty men here, I guarantee
that!

Tony laughing at me after saying
this.

His big brother, here with us today,
looking at us, wondering what we
werc talking about?

I explain to him, he is 10 years old,
by the way.

You see kiddo, woman do not come
here often.

"WHY?" The kiddo saying.

Because at this fair that we are at, a
bunch of boys here; let us say;
young men here, all believe they

are some character-from some
game of thrones slash robin hood
slash from some fairy tale land, that
every guy thinks that there is some
fair maiden out there who will
come here, and everyone will attack
her as if she is the hottest chick, in
all the land!

I was over selling it by a lot, to the
kiddo.

He had lost train of thought after I
said the word because, and I think I
just went on with the tangent, just
to be funny.

"I see a few females within the
land," Tony talking-renaissance.

"Okay brother, I am going to take
my sponsor here and we are going
to walk around and see what dorks
do at a renaissance fair," Walking
away from, leaving me be.

Wondering to myself, walking
around the fair, everything looked
cool.

People really did make this-
renaissance fair look like something
from one of those movies.

My eyes-catching the attention of
this castle-a few feet away from
me.

Walking towards it, the castle was
really detailed.

Someone built a wood structure,
making it seem like a real castle
was staring in front of you.

Seeing on each of the sides-of the
castle, I see two dudes, dressed up
as guards, but my question is why?

Why be guards here, wondering on
what they were guarding?

Then it happens?

A woman comes out from a peep
hole, must be a window of sort.

She-staring out into the blue-yonder
as if she was bored and such.

I step closer to get a better look-
staring up at her, she looks down at
me, smiling, saying hello next.

Hear ye Juliet, I say with a smile in
saying hello.

"I am not Juliet," Saying with a
paused look.

You are not?
Wondering what the hell she was
then.

"You did not look at the sign,
underneath my window," Pointing
that I look and read what the sign
says?

Reading it, it says; "Can you guess Rapunzel's hair length," Followed by; "All proceeds going to Mary's Heath Providence."

So, you are Rapunzel, and you are asking for donations, by hiding your hair and you want me to guess it?

Is this correct? Looking for validation.

"You are correct, so are you going to guess my hair length and let the next line of guys (Asking me to look behind me, noticing a bunch of nerds eagerly waiting in line to guess Rapunzel's hair length)"

Looking behind me it hits me?

This woman is hot, but my radar is turned off.

I think-this is because I am not searching for anyone and I am not

my brother, so, it's fine, I do not
care, telling my thoughts.

I guess your hair length is about, I
would say; 40 feet?

Throwing it out there.

She pulls her fake long hair out of
the window, and it was 20 feet, as
the marker had said on the fake
hair.

I guessed wrong I guess, I say.

"It is okay you guessed wrong."

"Your donation will help the
hospital that I work at."

I cannot wait to see a nurse; the
ultimate porn fantasy, saying in my
head.

Not saying this in real time, instead,
I pull out my wallet and hand her a

twenty-dollar bill, trying to reach
her hand with the money transfer.

Two of her guard subjects approach
me immediately, stopping me,
grabbing my hand, telling me to
step back away from the princess.

Is this really happening?
Telling my inner thoughts.

Can you tell me what did I do
wrong?

"You tried to touch the Queen's
hand, when you tried to hand her
the money," One of the guards
saying.

I did not know you would be in
trouble for doing this, I say
laughing.

"This is not funny!" The guard
saying.

"It is blasphemy!" The other guard
saying.

Okay, handing the guard the
money, proceeding to walk away.

"WAIT, YOUNG SIR," Rapunzel
calling out to me.

What's up my Queen, referencing
the joke back at her.

"What is your name?"

My name is Riley, Riley Admore.

What is your name Queen Bee,
giving her mad props!

"My name is Judith Praxton,
everyone calls me Judy for short."

Well, it was nice meeting you and I cannot wait until our paths-cross again, saying my goodbye.

"Sir, you must leave and let the others take there turns," The guard sounding demanding.

I smile, before walking away; making sure I get one more look at Judy before meeting up with my brother and his big brother.

"You saw a Queen and you did nothing but just give her a twenty-dollar bill?" Explaining this story to my produce manager; Larry, while he was near my station at self-checkout.

"Are you gay?" Larry asking next.

Looking at him, I feel the question had been asked-in form of another story somewhere?

Explaining to him; I am not gay,
and we just had a moment!

"Did you cyber stalk her yet?"

What do you mean?

"I mean, did you look her up on
social media and do your intel?"

What are you talking about?
Confused at what he was asking.

Crossing his arms, seeing he was
upset I did not get what he was
talking about?

"Let me explain to you boy,"
Crossing his arms when explaining.

"First thing, pull out your phone," I
pull it out, handing it to him.

"What is her name?"

Her name is Judith, but she goes by
Judy.

Putting the name Judith, Larry
scrolling around the name; Judith,
trying to see who would pop up.

Looking down on my phone,
scrolling and scrolling.

"She does not have a common
name, isn't that a bitch!" Handing
me my phone back.

"What, you need to do, when you
get off of work, is go on your
computer and find this girl and see
if you could make a connection of
sort."

Melissa walking up to us, Melissa
upset that I had not been watching

my station, instead talking to Larry
more, then paying attention.

Sorry Melissa, saying my exit to
Larry, going back to my station.

"Who are you stalking?"
My brother walking into my room
without saying anything.

I am not stalking brother; I was just
looking for some girl I saw at the
fair the other day.

"I saw like three wenches, which
ones were you looking at?"

She was in a castle.

"What castle?"

"The only woman I saw, they were
in the food court serving the food."

Well, this one, she was Rapunzel,
and her group took donations for
the hospital she worked at.

"Oh, you mean that line where all
the nerds were gathering at."

Yes, that one, I say to my brother.

"I did not get a good look at this
woman?"

"Was she hot!"

Right there after saying this, we
both; looking at Judith-staring in
front of our face.

That's her, looking at Tony.

"Dang, she looks like an-islander,
very beautiful!" Tony
complimenting.

"You were talking to that, and you
did not think once about asking for
her number?"

Tony scolding me.

I was trying to guess her hair
length, and I thought she was Juliet
from Romeo and Juliet.

"Are you-gay brother?"
"It is okay if you are," Putting an
arm around me.

You are the second person to ask
me this question today, you know.

"It says here she is living in the city
of Auburn, right next to us in
Kent!"

"What are the odds?" Tony
smirking when saying this.

Looking at her pictures, we did not
see any pictures with her and a guy,
you know, those standard pictures
of couples, where you see the same
two people in the same photo's-
indicating they were a couple.

She had a picture, dating back the
timeline, it was a year ago, but it
seems, it was only a few pictures.

"She probably scrubbed them?"

Scrubbed them, what does that
mean?

"It is, well, let us use me, for the
example brother."

I knew he was using this metaphor-
just so he could look up his ex-from
three years ago.

"Now, you see the beautiful ex of
mine," (Scrolling her pictures from
the past).

"If she had any pictures of me from
the past, they would be gone by
now, because she scrubbed them,
meaning she just erased me from
her life."

It had been three years ago since
my brother got dumped!

I know 100%, he is still not over
her and he probably looks her up on
social media, just to look at her
pictures.

I know 100%, his ex is married, and
I wish my brother would get over
her, but his way of getting over
someone, is why he dates so much!

That is his way of 100%, getting
over her; slowly getting over her.

"You are daydreaming brother," I
reply yes; yes, I was!

"The point I am trying to make
brother, is the point," (Changing
pictures to Judith's profile now).

"She probably has a few pictures
left of her ex-boyfriend because
maybe-there is still something
there?"

What do I care? Saying with a
smile.

"If she is single, like really, really
single; she would not have any
pictures of her ex; kind of like how
my ex has no pictures of me,
anymore on any of her timeline,"
Tony walking away, making his
way to the kitchen.

Looking at her picture one last
time, I got to see a few pictures she
took posing as Rapunzel.

She was beautiful, but my radar
was not in the mood for trying to
find me a date or something.

Texting some of the friends at
work, we were planning a surprised
baby shower for one of our
managers, as a surprise.

After getting all the details, I go
into the kitchen to get some ice
water to lay on my stand next to my
bed, I see my brother singing,
clearly, he was three sheets to the
wind.

"Brother!"

Tony pouring me some gin, pouring
some sprite with it, before handing
it to me.

I wanted to say no thank you, I was
not feeling it, but I know my
brother was hurting from the
viewing of his ex from earlier.

The music was playing loudly from
his phone, my brother starting to
sing.

"Oh, I,"
Starting to dance around the
kitchen.

"Baby what a fool I am,"
"First a boy and then a man, am I,"

"And you, you're the heart of it
all,"

"You're the things I say and do,"

"Am I wasting my time,"
Now sitting in the kitchen chair,
tears starting to come down.

"But I can't help it,"

"Every moment,"
Tony's voice cracking, I come sit
next to him, arm around him,
comforting him.

"Love, take away,,,,,,"

Crying now in my arms.

Putting him in the shower, before
tucking him into bed.

I sleep with him to make sure he
was feeling safe and warm.

Love?

Love makes the world go round and
I am glad I have nothing to be a
part of it right now.

You can do Magic

In my 29 years of living, I have heard many stories about how one person meets-their future spouses and working at a grocery store, I am always in the know, of how so many people meet and it amazes me at how their stories are so cool!

Channel, the girl who we are giving that secret baby shower party too, she met her husband; Roy; one day, back in 1998, when the two met in the 11th grade at their High School.

Always wondering how, wondering
at history?

Channel saying-Roy was talking to
another girl, when the other girl
dumped him; he was standing by
the front of the school, waiting for
his parents to pick him up, she so
happened to be there with him, the
two talked and that was that!

Larry in produce told me he met his
wife here at the store.

I asked how?

"She was a customer shopping!"

"That was how!"
Larry saying sarcastically back at
me.

In the break room, Melissa sitting
by herself, I sit next to her, in the
open seat.

How are you doing, saying
casually.

Eating a piece of chicken, offering
me some from her bag; she tells me
she met someone outside when she
went out for a smoke.

What's his name?

"Eddie Garland."

Does he seem okay?

"He asked to bum a cigarette and
told me he had seen me many times
in the store, and he seemed
normal."

"He is cute, I tell you that much."

When are you two going to go out?

"We are going to-TJ's Grill by the mall Friday night."

"Are you okay with me going out with him," Melissa asking me quietly, so nobody else around us could hear us.

It's fine Melissa.

You can go out with whoever you want to?

Continuing to eat her chicken, I look at the clock, noticing my ten-minute break was over, I had to man the customer service desk downstairs.

Working customer service was a bit hard for me to learn at first but then I got the hang of it when my teacher, her name-Gloria!

Gloria taught me a lot about the customer service world.

One big thing I did learn from the start; everyone loved to play the lottery at my store.

I was never into the lottery but after meeting the regular cliental, I got to learn on what person had their addictions with?

After that, everything else went great!

When my shift had ended, I usually offered Melissa a ride home because she lived on the way to my home but tonight, she did not come up to me-asking if I would give her a ride?

I did not think nothing of it, I just went in my car, started it, came home; showered, un-winded- by watching television before going into bed.

Waking up that night around three am, the dead hour as the world calls it.

Scrolling on Judith's profile, I see- she was visiting the Kubota Gardens with her parents.

Taking photos in front of the beautiful flowers and taking a photo of herself praying in front of one of the statues.

Stunning as usual; right now, would be the perfect moment to like her photo and give her that validation of how awesome her pictures looked.

I do not know her though?

This is where I would be labeled a creeper-if I was to like her photo.

Going to the message part of the app, I tell myself to send her a message and say hi, how are you doing, how have you been?

Hoping maybe next-she would
respond?

Ah hell, telling myself.

I write the first message to start the
conversation, in hopes I guess, I
hope to see where this goes?

Message first.

Hi, you probably do not remember
me, I was at the renaissance fair,
and I donated twenty bucks to the
cause; message sent.

…..
Indicating the message being sent.

The next box indicating with a
check mark, indicating she got the
message.

Staring at the message, waiting to see if she would reply to the message?

3 am; I do not think she would reply to the message?

I fall asleep, putting my phone on the stand.

In the morning I wake up and to my surprise the bubble shows-she seen the message.

But, she did not reply?

This-funny to me.

So, my next thoughts were-she probably read the message, said to herself; "I remember him?"

Then just said nothing else after the matter.

"You did not say a word back to her
after seeing she had clearly read
your message?"

Larry from Produce saying.

I did not know what else should I
say to her?

"You could have said thanks for
reading my message and would you
like to have some coffee
sometime?"

I told you Larry, I am not wanting
to date anyone right now.

"So, would you rather be alone at
night, or would you rather have
someone to talk with in the
nighttime,"

Giving me that stare, wondering if I
knew what he was talking about?

I understand what you are saying
Larry.

"I am wondering if you are,"
Staring back at me.

Pulling out my phone, going into
my apps messages I show him;
here, I type to Judith; how is your
day going, leaving with the
question mark.

We both stare which felt like
eternity!

Before clocking out of my shift, I
stare at my phone once more and I
see I have a message.

I look at it and I see the bubble over
the message, indicating she has read
the message.

Like a little kid being excited,
inside the car, I have the biggest
smile on my face.

It all goes down next because I
wonder next on why she did not
message me back, just looking at
the message rather than message
back?

ECC IS THE PLACE TO BE

Happy to sleep in today; it was not going to happen sadly!

My brother barges in, looking at me; telling me to wake up!

Looking back at him, I tell him it was 9:00am, so why would I wake up right now, especially when it was a day off from work?

"I know you might be mad at me for waking you up brother, but we have somewhere to be,"

Saying; acting as if I knew-we were
going somewhere?

Where are we going? I ask
wondering.

He throws a green lantern unitard at
me, with the mask for the eyes!

And what is this, I ask wondering?

"Well, my big brother with me, is
in the living room."

"He is the yellow lantern-wearing
the yellow unitard and I am, as you
can see; am the red-lantern, wearing
the red unitard!"

"So, brother, guess which lantern
you are?"
Looking at me.

I guess I am the Green Lantern, I
say with a smile.

Getting ready, my brother walks
into my bathroom handing me the
green ring, the thing to complete
the costume.

Putting on the eye mask, I like it, I
say to him.

Where is this place we are going
too?

"They hold this Comic Con thing in
downtown Seattle every year and
the big brother place had four
tickets they gave out and I told
them I could use an extra ticket, for
you to go with us."

"It will be fun because for one day,
in this big ass building-will be in,
there will be all these people
dressed up in their favorite
costumes and you will get to see all
your favorite super-heroes in one
building!"

What was the reasoning for being
the lantern character?

"The kid going with us-had his
wish of wanting to go to this place
for a couple of years."

"The big brother place got tickets
for free this year and so here we
are!"

Having no idea what this was, it
was a trip when we got there.

So many people dressed up,
dressing up as their favorite
characters from television shows
we grew up too, some dressing into
movie star characters from all the
comic book movies.

Not realizing we were dressed up as
well, I felt normal in this building;
walking around, everyone that saw
us, seeing me; giving me a smile, I
give them a smile back.

Taking pictures with people who wanted to be in a photo with the three of us.

I liked how we stood out, feeling somewhat important!

My brother did a good thing by dragging me out today for this event.

Walking through the merch isle, his big brother- wanted some comic books of some character that I had no idea about?

Walking to where the shirts were, I wanted to see if I could find something cool to buy and wear later in life.

I see a girl wearing a costume, looking like Dorothy from The Wizard of Oz.

Only seeing the back of her, I see
her hair in the braids, I see the dress
spot on, along with some cool
bedazzled looking shoes.

This cosplayer (Saying to my
thoughts).

She was really-spot on, with the
costume!

Looking to the side of her, I see one
person dressed up as the cowardly
Lion and one dressed up as the
monkey from the Witches brood.

I walk back to let Tony and his big
brother know about this costume I
had just scene.

We got to get a picture with these
cosplayers!
I say excitedly!

We head towards them, I get my
phone out; I ask the woman if I
could have a picture with her; she,
turning around, we both looking at
each other, I pause!

It is you, Judith!
I say with a big smile.

"You are?"
Not recognizing me it seems.

It's Riley, I say with a smile, before
taking my eye mask off.

"Oh hi!"
Giving me a hug next.

"I did not recognize you," She
apologizes.

"Great costume!"

Thank you, I say back.

My brother, introducing her to him,
she-shaking his hand and shaking
his big brother sponsors hand as
well.

"What is your costume?"
Tony's big brother asking.

He is only 9, he does not know
anything about The Wizard of Oz.

Her Monkey and Lion; the two
guards I had met at the castle from
before, both saying hi, shaking my
hand next.

You guys like the ECC too?
I ask.

"We have been coming here every
year for the past six-years!" Judith
proudly saying.

We are here, for my brother's big
brother wish, they gave us three
tickets and I was asleep, and they
woke me up to come here.

"GREAT TIMING!" Judith saying.

Her friends wanting to have lunch
now, both of our groups had been
walking around for a few hours
already.

Can we join you for lunch?
Asking without thinking.

Judith saying yeah, I have no
problem with that.

Walking into the kitchen made area
in the building, it was like a scene
from our days in High School,
where you are lining up with a tray,
you have your fork, your spoon,
your cup, and you get in line.

But the cool part of this High
School, you are in a lunch line
where you are in line with a
cosplayer, each person next to you,

wearing different costumes around you!

It was so cool; I was enjoying the whole moment and great vibes of the place.

Sitting down at a table, everyone talking with one another, everyone mingling.

Judith switches seats with someone, wanting to sit next to me, she wanted to talk.

"I wanted to apologize on why I never responded to any of your messages," Saying quietly to me.

I understand if you are busy, it's quite alright.

"Well, I know men can get upset if a girl just looks at the message, but

says nothing, because you know
how men tend to get weird about
it.”

I totally understand!

Looking for you online was kind of
hard because you never gave me
any clues?

“Was-I suppose too?”
She asks wondering.

Oh no, saying back.

I only knew your name was Judith
and I just looked online-on the
media-app and I found you.

It said you live in Auburn.

“I do,”
“Where do you live?”

I live in Kent.

I live with the Red Lantern,
pointing him out; him, looking back
at me with that smile, indicating he
was rooting for me, I guess, saying
to my thoughts.

"You saw my castle I was in; it was
for a charity, and I am a nurse there,
and I am always busy!"

You do not have to explain yourself
for ghosting me, saying this as a
joke to her.

"I did not mean to ghost you,"
saying with a smile.

"I was just busy!"

I understand, I really do, giving her
a smile back when saying.

Our eyes both then notice the same
thing across from our table.

"This is Gospel!" She says to me.

Yes, this is Gospel, and I
understand the song lyric.

"You do?" Smiling at me.

Who does not-Panic at the disco!

I used to rock their songs on Rock
Band, back in the day.

It seems there was this era back in
2007-2010, when we all thought we
could be Guitar Players and we all
played the games well.

"I know, I remember those times
well!" Judith reminiscing with her
thought's.

"We have to go and get closer-to
see if they will let us take a picture
with them?"

"What are you two talking about?"
Tony putting an-arm around my
neck, wondering what we were
starstruck on?

That is Big Daddy and Little sister,
explaining to my brother.

Looking at me, wanting to know
what the heck we were talking
about?

Judith chiming in with how these
cosplayers were two characters
from a great game from back in the
day.

"I have no idea what you two are
talking about?" Tony lost.

Anyways brother, getting up to my
feet, reaching a hand-out for Judith;
she takes hold, we both walk, hand

and hand-slowly feeling as if we
were both meeting our favorite
celebrity.

Walking nervously, I whisper to
Judith; who do you want a picture
with the most?

The Big Daddy or the little Sister?

"Both!" She whispers back to me.

Hello, I say, the two-eating a couple
of sandwiches.

The Big Daddy, his helmet off but
his armor on.
I had to ask him-how did he get all
this stuff made?

"Easy!" Saying nonchalantly.

"Me and my wife," Looking at the
Little Sister.

"We like to go to all these events
and the game you see us-
Cosplaying too; this is our favorite
game of all time!"

Me too!
Me too!

Judith and me saying at the same
time.

The game was so amazing back
when, right?

Reminding myself of how great the
game was.

"You two have some amazing
costumes yourself," Big Daddy
complimenting us.

Explaining the situation, ending
with; I did not know Judith would
be here as Dorothy.

"How long have you two been
together?"

Oh, I am sorry, we are not a couple,
I say with a smile-staring at Judith.

She smiles back, not feeling
offended at all.

We get our pictures taken, first as
them in their costumes together.

Second, we get individual pictures
where Judith and me, reveling in all
of this!

After the photo shoot was done, I
give them each a twenty-dollar bill,
thanking them for the moment!

"No problem, dude," Hitting my
shoulder-playfully like.

Walking back to the table, Tony
and his big brother said it was time
to explore more of the comic con
place.

Sure, I said.

Wondering now if me and Judith
were to part?

"We could walk with you guys, if
you want?" Judith saying.

Prayers answered, saying to my
inner thoughts.

The six of us walking around, we
saw so many cool things.

I enjoyed the whole moment, but
the moment did not last long when I
found out the real reason on why
we were here?

I was starting to wonder about thirty minutes ago when I noticed my brother kept looking at his phone for no reason and he kept randomly looking down on it, here and there.

And nothing wrong with that, but whenever he looked down on it, we suddenly were moving into a new direction of this place.

Finally, after moving this way and that way, we were by the merchant booths again; I was ready to pull him aside and tell him; why did we come back to this area again?

I did not need to say anything, because seeing him look forward, I looked forward at whatever he was looking at.

Sadly, I saw what he was looking at?

Judith walking closer to me, whispering; "What is going on?"

"Why are we stopping?"

Looking at my brother, I walk to
him; what the hell are we doing
here?

Slightly, yelling in his ear, while
looking at what he was looking at
in front of us.

"What do you mean brother?" Tony
ignoring my question.

Putting my hand to his cheek,
making him look at me, I ask him
again; Why the hell are we looking
at your ex-girlfriend, here at ECC!

Tony, not saying nothing back to
me.

I pull him aside, away from
everyone to ask him again.

Why, are we looking at your ex-
girlfriend that is here!

I demand him to answer me now!

Judith, seeing what was going on,
she and her two friends,
disappearing from us.

The big brother, having no idea
what was going on?

I see my brother's ex-girlfriend,
turning around; her current
husband, putting a hand onto her
stomach, telling me now-this was
why, we were here?

Explaining to Judith in message
form, I apologize for the second
time, explaining we had a situation
and we had to take care of it.

She messages back; "What
happened?"

What happened was after we
dropped off his big brother, I asked
my brother-why did we run into his
ex at the comic con.

"Because brother," He started off
with.

"Have you ever been in love, where
it hurts every day, knowing no
matter how your day ends, when
you wake up, she is no longer there
and as each thing time-passing, you
will realize; she is never coming
back!"

During this drive I could
understand how my brother was
feeling.

I wondered though, how did he
know?

The big brother place never gave
you the tickets, did they?

"No brother, the did not."

How did you get them?

"I bought them from an online
vendor when I saw her post, after
her and her husband announced
they were having a baby girl this
summer."

I understand brother how we still
get attached to people, like-how we
slowly grieve when something ends
and then something new begins!

"I tried to forget about her, I really
did brother."

"You know that song; don't ever be
lonely, by the Cornelius Brothers
and Sister Rose?"

Yeah, I know that song, saying
back.

"I play that song in my head, over
and over again!"

It is not fair for you to feel
miserable brother!

We break up, we move on, that
should be it!
I argue back.

"For you maybe, but for me it is not
like that!"

"Your brother must have really
loved her?" Judith messaging next.

This is the messed-up part-to this
equation.

"How so?"

When my brother and her were
together, she was always mean to
him?

That is what I do not get?

When they were together, he would
tell me how he would open the door
for her and she would get mad at
him and say- "Gosh, every time!"

And I would be like, she did not
want you to open her doors?

"Yeah!" My brother would say.

(Judith just listening towards each
thing I said, not responding.)

He would be complimenting her
every day on her looks, telling her

how beautiful she was and how
everyday he was happy to just see
her.

She would get mad at him, telling
him she felt smothered!

I never understood how a woman
refused any good comments,
especially my brother, who was not
a mean guy, but she never wanted
his lines?

"It happens?" Judith messaging
back.

"I hate to end this conversation, but
I have to look over some patients,"
Messaging ending.

I thank her for chatting with me,
even though now, looking at my
watch on the laptop, it saying it was
3:32am, who would not be cool to
think a nurse would be messaging
me this early in the morning.

Permanent Stay

"So, you are going to be more in customer service now," Larry asking.

Something like that?

It seems two more people quit, so, I get the bump in pay, but now I have to-be here more, than be a cashier and at self checkout, you know?

"What job do you like the best out of the three?"

I do not know right now!

All I know is, changes are coming
to the store and people are always
leaving and new management keeps
coming in.

How do you manage to stay here
Larry?

"I shut my mouth, do my job, and
that is it!"

Walking away then.

An hour left in my shift, Melissa;
who was the managing supervisor
for the shift right now, she walks
over to me asking if I wanted to
take my lunch now?

I say yeah, why not!

Walking away now.

She stops me then, asking if I had a
few seconds?

Sure, what's up?

Waiting on her to answer, looking
at her, her eyes looking to the side;
she was not saying anything, so I
walked away, taking my break, not
saying a word.

In the break room, I look on my
phone, seeing a message from
Judith.

She put her phone number in it this
time.

 A Plus, on my end; thinking?

I have earned the right to text her
now, what a great right to earn!

Adding her number to my contacts,
the rest of my shift I was on this
high, where I just was so happy, my
friends at work, all looking at me,
wondering why I was so happy.

I kept it to myself, coming home.

Later that night I was looking at her pictures on social media when Tony walks in; seeing what I was seeing, he ask's if I liked any of the photo's yet?

Not yet, saying back.

A great thing had just happened earlier at work brother, boasting about it now.

"What happened?"

"Did they promote you again?"

No, nothing like that.

Judith messaged me her phone number brother.

"That is freaking great!"
"Proud of you brother!"

"Did you text her yet?"

NOPE!

"Why the hell not?"

"She gave you the okay by giving
you, her number!"

"Freaking call-her brother!"

Looking down at my phone
scrolling to her name, I could not
call her right now?

Something inside me just telling me
not to text her.

Pointing at her pictures, Tony told
me to look at the last three that
were posted within the last few
days.

"Do you know what they call those
pictures brother?"

No, what do they call them?

"Dirty Selfies, brother!"

What does that mean? I have no
idea what he meant.

"What I mean brother; two weeks
ago, if you look at her pictures,
those were before we saw her at the
fair and at the comic con."

Your point being?

"My point being brother, she is
showing pictures of how sexy she
looks because she is trying to send
that bat-signal out to every guy who
wants to try their luck and get to
know her?"

"The pictures are not meant for her
to show some skin and want men to
drool over her brother."

"The point is, she just sent the bat signal, and you need to answer it!"

I do not know how brother?

I was really being true about this statement.

It has been a while and I know this one is not a coke head, laughing with him.

My brother pulls up his phone showing me a place he wanted me to ask her out too.

"This weekend, the farmers market at that park in Federal Way," Him, saying.

"Ask her out for a walk there, have lunch there; coffee, some scones; you two will have a great time, brother!"

How are you doing brother,
throwing the question back at him.

"I am making it brother, that is all I
could tell you right now."

"Every day can be an-obstacle," All
he said next.

SEVEN LONG DAYS LATER…..

She took a ride share while I drove
to the farmer's market.

Walking towards me, she wore this
floral print dress; stunning,
beautiful dress; no sleeves,
sunglasses, a hat to match the
whole-esemble.

Her shoes were sandals-looking like
Egyptian ones.

Walking up to me first, she gave me
a kiss on the cheek-in saying hello.

Her lips touching my face, you
know you could feel that warmth
when you feel something so right,
touching you, exactly at that right
moment!

Thank you for coming out today
and spending time with me, looking
at her; just admiring the beautiful
day as a bonus with the two of us
here.

Walking around the vendors, I pick
up a flower from the first flower
vendor I see; quickly handing it to
her.

Smiling behind her dark glasses, I
did not even think, but I just held
her free hand and we walked and

talked, walking past vendors and
such.

She told me work has been very
busy, she had been taking more
shifts to help the workload with her
peers at the hospital.

A few days ago, my brother joked
about how the number one fantasy
for any man, was to be dating a
nurse, because it seemed like every
fantasy began with a nurse!

I laughed at this and told him I
respect every job any woman does.

Pouring some more drink into his
cup, he walks back into his room,
closing the door behind him.

In the present now, I asked Judith a
little about her story and how she
came here?

"My story is simple," Saying with a
smile.

"I was born in Des Moines."
"My father was a doctor in Federal
Way."

"When I was in High School, I
wanted to learn more about what
my dad did."

Why was that?

"My dad would come home late at
night, he would be so tired, but I
would hear him in the kitchen,
talking to my mom about all the
stuff he had gone through that day."

"He loved his patients, he loved
helping everyone at his job!"

"My mother and him would always
talk in the kitchen after each night,
thinking to myself how nice."

"How nice it was to be in love like
that!"

Have you ever been in love like
that?
I ask wondering.

"Have you?"
Throwing the question back at me.

I have not been in love like that, but
I can tell you, my brother has been
in love like that; seeing him in love,
seeing him with the stars at his feet.

It is a great feeling seeing
something beautiful, feeling the
world at your feet!

"Why did your brother and his ex-
not get married?"

The moment never got to be-
because the two always fought!

I always wondered how could-he
say now, how happy he was, but at
the time when they were together,
they just fought and fought!

I know now-if things were bad, but
for him, he was in this love circle.

"I know what you mean?"

You do?

"Of course," Saying with a smile.

She understood what I was talking
about, put a smile to my face.

The rest of the day was just
amazing!

Before saying goodbye, she asked if
I was going to use a ride share for a
ride back home?

I told her I had my own car here;
she was welcome to let me drive
her home?

The sun setting, her shades off.

She gives me a look, thinking about
the offer?

She walks up to me, hugging me,
before saying her ride is here.

Lost in The 50's Tonight!

Getting ready, my costume tonight
was not a costume of a comic book
character.

My costume tonight was a costume
where I was a greaser, kind of like
that guy from the greaser movie.

Why, was I dressed like this
tonight?

Having the leather jacket, having
the white t-shirt underneath;
finishing the outfit off with tight
jeans and black boots to match?

The local rotary club here in
Renton, doing a 1950's themed
Dance, being held for charity.

Since the farmers market-I asked
Judith a few days ago if she would
come join me at this event.

Larry, an ex-Army soldier, told me
about the event.

Telling me he had two tickets to
pawn off for the charity, the
proceedings going to the wounded
warrior project.

He asked me first, walking up to
my line while I was being a cashier
today.

"I got these two-tickets to paradise
friend!" Starting off with the joke.

What are the tickets for?

"My rotary club at the VFW in Puyallup, are giving us each VA members-two tickets a piece to sell, for outside people to come to this ball."

What kind of ball?

"It's a themed ball my friend!"

"We are going back to the early days of Rock N Roll."

Which is?

"The 1950's, my boy!" Putting the tickets on my check stand.

"50 buck's friend!" Saying with a laugh.

Handing him the cash, I look over to customer service seeing Melissa manning the desk.

She looks at me, I look back at her with a smile.

Larry, rolling his eyes at me.

"Stay away from that, and you know-I do not have to explain myself," Taking the money and walking away from me.

Texting Judith during break, I know it had been a few weeks since the walk at the farmers market, we did not text much after that time.

Feeling kind of stupid for just texting her out of the blue, asking her if she wanted to go to a VFW function.

"Sure," Without question, texting back in a hurry.

"What is the function?"

We are going to be living in the 1950's-for one night, texting proudly thru text.

"Groovy, I cannot wait to go."

A ride share pulling up to the VFW,
Larry smoking next to me, I ask
him; have you heard anything about
second-hand smoke?

Laughing at me, puffing another
smoke from his cigarette.

Judith coming out of the car, poodle
skirt, pink, pink shirt-lace thing, her
hair in-pony tail-like fashion; my
eyes just fixated at how beautiful
she was looking.

Larry hits my shoulder with a tap;
"Oh please do not fuck this up!"
Walking away from me.

Hi, I say first; she says hi back,
followed by a kiss on my cheek
again.

I could have-picked you up, if you
had texted me directions, sounding
desperate, even when saying this

without thinking; it did sound
desperate.

She ignored the question, took hold
of a hand and we walked into the
VFW.

The whole place was decked out
with all the 1950's greats, gracing
the walls in portraits.

They went all out, looking at Judith,
looking at her amazement when
seeing her gleeful smile, amazed
just like how I was feeling when
seeing it all together as one.

"Shall we get some punch?" Judith
asking.

Sure, I say, walking with her to the
beverage tray.

"Do you two want spiked punch or
do you two just want regular- the
regular Kool-Aid," The bartender
asking us.

"Spike us!" Judith saying with a
smile.

Lady calls it, I say to the bartender.

Taking our sips, our eyes meeting
before that first sip, hitting our lips,
the stuff was good!

Finishing our cups, Judith, having
some black-looking glasses, pulled
from in between her outfit, she tells
me she bought these earlier-to
complete her outfit.

It did not matter-glasses or no
glasses, Judith was hot, and she was
here with me tonight!

The first song coming on was
Chubby Checker's; Twist again!

The two of us dancing as if we
knew the song well.

You know how this song reference
is? I ask wondering.

"Of course, I do!"

You do?

"Yes Riley, I do!"

Explaining to me she listened to
oldies on one of her stations on her
phone and she knew about the song
and how you dance to it as if you
are putting out a cigarette.

Right there, I wanted to marry her-
right there and then!
We danced to that song first, then
the next song; "Peppermint Twist!"

We twisted, we shaked our groove
thing!

We were having a blast!

The place was packed on the dance
floor, seeing all the other people
dancing around us.

After a few more fast songs, a slow
song, the "DJ" Announcing it was
time to slow it down.

Playing the song; "True Love
Ways," Buddy Holly!

Holding Judith-arm and arm;
staring into her eyes, I ask her if she
knows about Buddy Holly?

She nods a no.

It is a beautiful story; would you
like to hear about it?

"Sure Riley, do tell me the story."

The story starts off in the city of
Lubbock, Texas, where he came
from.

He played a mean guitar and he died by the time he was 22, in a plane crash.

"This, this is a sad story."

It is in a way, but there is a great love story!

"There is?"

Yes, I say.

He was married to a woman and when he met her, he married her immediately!

"Why so quickly?" Judith wondering.

I do not know the reasoning behind it, but I remember I read a story where he met her and then asked her after a few days if they could get married and she said; "I do not even know you well," Or something like that?

They were married and he died!

Hugging me, pulling in closer, the
song, all I could think about-was
how the violin part of the song
swayed to the music-just about-in
the right way, the two of us were
having a great time.

When reality hitting, looking
around my surroundings, I see
Larry; Larry tipping his cup to me, I
think this was his way of saying;
"Good Job boy, good job," Or
something sarcastic?

Sitting at a table, the meal served
for us here tonight, hot dogs or
burgers, with fries or onion rings.

I walked back to the punch guy,
Judith's request-asking we get some
more of that spiked Kool Aide!

Got to honor any Queen's request
right! Saying this to my head.

After our food, feeling a little
stuffed, Larry comes over to
introduce himself and introduce his
wife, Candance.

I did not know an ass can be
married, saying this as a joke.

"Easy there, killer!"

"I am the one with the jokes
tonight!"

Shaking hands with Judith after
introducing her, the four of us talk,
finishing our food, we go back on
the dance floor to dance to some
more music.

As it got later in the night, when the
next slow song came on, it was
Bobby Helm's; "You are my
Special Angel!"

Judith was very tipsy, I can feel her
holding me, loosing her grip-every
so often.

Are you okay, I ask her, looking
into her eyes, seeing she was
starting to fall asleep in my arms!

I walk her to the outside, telling her
it was time for us to go home.

Her eyes closing in and out.

I have my car here, let's take you
home I say, walking her slowly into
the passenger side.

Tucking her head in gently.

Putting the seatbelt on her, I walk
over to the driver side, Judith
completely passed out, her head
slumped over, I had to find a way
of figuring out how to get her
home-she never gave me her
address?

Looking at her purse, I was not
going to go that route!

Her head, starting to move, leaning
towards me, her lips, basically right
there for the taking; she pulls out
her phone; saying next to the
operator on the hands-free button,
"Take me to 12345, Sheridin Drive,
Auburn, Washington!"

Her phone pulling the map app,
directing me next, I put her phone
on my hands-free set, driving us to
her home.

We get to a gate.

A gated community (Telling my
thoughts).

I have no way of entering the code
because she is passed out-right next
to me (Telling my inner thoughts
again).

Thinking of what to do?

A car pulling up, heading into the
keypad driveway, I look at them,
they look back at me.

"Hey bro," The driver saying.

"Is that Judith asleep in your car?"
Asking.

Yes, it is I say, hoping they knew
her.

A door opens, a couple people, a
male and female, coming out to
inspect on Judith.

"Is she okay?" The woman asking.

Yeah, she is fine.
She is just tired.

We were at a 1950's dance at the
VFW in Puyallup, and Judith got a
little tipsy, but all it did was make
her sleep, so, here we are.

The man, opening her side of the
car, the woman unbuckling her.

"Thank you for bringing her back
here, we can take her home," The
woman saying.

You all know her?

"Of course, I know her," Saying
with a smile.

"I am her sister," She and the other
men, carrying her into there car, the
gate opening, myself saying
goodbye.

A Night in the Nursery

"You never thought about kissing her?" Larry asking.

The moment was there, but she was asleep!

You guys over there (Referring to his gang of Army exes-at the VFW).

You guys know how to throw one dam-good party! (Complimenting Larry).

˙"I told you-you would have a good
time with us."

"What happened when you took her
home?"

You saw her in my car?

"I saw Riley,"
"I saw!"

Nothing happened though.

I took her to her place, she lived in
a gated community, I did not have
the passcode to open the gate.

"So, what happened?"

A car pulled up, it happened to be
her sister in the car, they took her
sleeping body away, like sleeping
beauty.

"How did you sleep then?"

(Larry trying to dig into something
else?)

I slept okay, if that is what you are
asking, but I think I know what
your smart-ass, is trying to inquire?

(Knowing, I know exactly what he
wanted me say back to him.)

I would not give him the
satisfaction to the question.

Later in the night, it was around
9:00pm, getting ready to close my
eyes, a message comes in from the
app.

"You did not call me-to see if I was
okay or not?"
Judith saying, sounding a bit upset
about it.

Texting-instead of going through
the message app, I tell her, it was

nice meeting your sister, but I did
not get her name.

"Her name is Vivi, short for
Vivian!"

"She says you were pretty cute, all
worried about me, when waiting at
the gate, looking like a lost puppy,
not knowing what to do in the
situation?"

I knew what to do, texting her back
immediately, joking-she thought I
was lost?

"Are you-busy right now?" Judith
texting back.

I was about to go to sleep, why?
Is there something you want to ask
of me?

"My unit at the hospital is having a
mini party in the ward, and I was
wondering if you wanted to come
and be my plus +1?"

"I am working the night shift tonight, so, I understand if you are busy?"

An hour later, heading up to the floor she worked at, she was sitting in a chair, looking down at her phone.

I say hi to her, excitedly!

Looking up at me, I pant a little, breathing a little hard, trying to get myself together.

She, in her scrubs, looking more sexier than ever; she hugs me a hello; before smiling, wondering why didn't I text her back?

When you said you wanted me to come to this party, I quickly got dressed and got ready and raced my butt over here so, I could see, see you right now, as I see you, in your scrubs, explaining.

Hugging me!

I made sure I did not break from her
embrace until she let me go!

She introduces me to her ward, I
meet doctors, I meet other nurses.

We get some cake and some ice
cream.

"Would it be okay if you helped me
pass some of the cake and ice
cream to the patients in the ward?"
(Asking me as if I would ever say
no, of which I did not).

After we shared cake and ice cream,
we went to each ward on the floor,
giving ice cream and cake.

Meeting the patients, I was happy
to know a lot about them and Judith
explained to me-for everyone we
passed, there story, there bios.

She knew everyone's story, she
treated everyone like they were her
own child, with the kids in the
ward.

One sad thing though about this
cake and ice cream moment?

The ward she was working at, the
ward was the ward where all the-
very sickly people within the city
were at.

Aids, Cancer; others dying from
other ailments; Judith introduces
me to all of them!

By the fifteenth person, my
stomach starting to turn, she assures
me-all is well; and how most of
these people are happy to meet God
someday, if they never get to leave
the ward.

So passionate about the job I
commend her.

After delivering the last bit of cake
and ice cream, she tells me; there is
a silver lining to this place.

What is the lining, I ask?

She takes my shoulder, leaning into
it, we go on the elevator, a couple
floors down; we are now in the
maternity ward, where all the new
babies are in the incubators.

"This is where life begins," Judith
whispering to my left ear.

"This is where it all begins, and
these babies are the future and the
next generation of lives to be
living!"

"I come down here at times to
remind myself from the ward, to
just tell myself-life is beautiful!"

Awesome, complimenting her.

She looks at me, I look at her.

I wonder if this was the moment to
kiss her.

Larry looking at me weird when
explaining me to this.

"That should have been the moment
then to kiss?"

I just did not want to do it, arguing
back.

Watching the shower, the timing on
the vegetables, seeing them getting
sprayed, I look at Larry and I tell
him how the rest of the night ends.

"Something tells me, it ends with
you being alone in your bed?"
Larry laughing.

The sun was rising, you could see
the shadow of day light starting to
creep in.

I stayed up all night with you it
seems, smiling at her when saying
this.

"It seems that you did," Giving me
a hug back.

Walking me to the elevator, we
both look at each other once more, I
had no words to really say back to
her-other than I had a really good
time hanging out with her.

She gave me a look!

"A look?"
"And you did nothing!"

Yes Larry, I did nothing, again.

"It seems you are in your own
Rom-con?"

Whatever it was, I like what I am
in, before walking back to my self-
checkout station.

"Wait?" Larry stopping me.

What's up?

"Before you met Judith, do you
remember when you first started
working here and a few months in,
there was this girl that always came
in your line-when you were
checking, and you never had the
galls to ask for her name?"

Yeah, I remember her.

"You never talk about her
anymore?"
"Why?"

The story ended because one day,
while being in self-checkout, she
bought alcohol and I got to find out
her name.

It was Beth, like the cat persona
from KISS!

I remember when seeing her, I was
like a quiet-low key stunned person,
who could not speak!

I remember I could talk with any
stranger but when I saw her, I
would freak out and be quiet-like
that Charlie Brown episode where
he kept seeing that mysterious
woman-but could not do anything
about it!

"Judith was the path then?"

Maybe she was?

"RILEY?" Melissa calling out to
me.

Excusing myself, I ask her what's up?

"You have been away from self-checkout, and I was wondering where you disappeared too?"

I was just talking to Larry in Produce.

"That is not what I was referring too?" Melissa saying.

Confused at the question, it hit me suddenly, realizing she was talking about something else?

Is there something you want to talk to me about after work?

"Yes, can you give me a ride home afterwards," Asking.

Two hours later, parked outside, the two of us sitting quietly in the car.

I waited for her to say something,
but I think she wanted me to say
something instead.

"We do not talk anymore, like how
we used too, remember?" Melissa
asking.

I understand what she was saying.

We did not talk much anymore
because-we were going in two
different directions at the store.

I did not know what else to say-but
I just asked that we end our
conversation so I could head home
already?

She gave me an-upset face look
before slamming my door in saying
goodbye!

Finally, home, it was almost 1am;
thinking to myself last night I was
at a ward with Judith, looking at
sickly patients and passing cake and
ice cream to them.

Walking into the kitchen, my
brother was sitting down, drink-in
his hand.

What's going on brother?

Noticing me now, he said he was
celebrating tonight?

What were you celebrating?

"Before you get mad at me brother,
I met up with her!"

With who?
Not understanding the question.

"With Jennifer!"

With your ex?
The one we saw at ECC?

"Yes brother, my ex, we saw at
ECC."

Where did you see her at?

"I was getting gas and her car
pulled up next to me, like a scene
from a movie!"

She had no idea brother-you got a
new car, I say.

"Yeah, she had no idea, so, it was
one of those amazing moments
where you see the woman of your
dreams and you just want to tell
her-everything you have been
thinking of, so, when the time
comes, you could tell her
everything!"

Did you get to tell her everything?

"Of course not!"

"I get to the part where I say hello,
and everything I had been building
up to say to her, it all disappears
from my brain-because I notice her
baby bump, also noticing the ring
on her finer; the gentleman way of
doing things, I tell her; congrats and
pump my gas and everything I had
been thinking about?"

"All of it lost now!"

Pouring the refill in his glass.

I pick him up, leaving the refilled
glass, I walk him into the room,
taking off his shoes, his socks, I
tuck him into his bed; he falls
asleep immediately.

Asleep, I wake up a few hours later,
heading into the restroom, looking
at my phone on the counter, I see a
text message from Judith.

She sent me a text with a selfie in
front of her desk, she-looking
amazing!

The End....

Thank you for reading book #2 of
the four, in the series of the vision!

See you next in book #3   "Pauper's
Delight!"

9 798847 251716